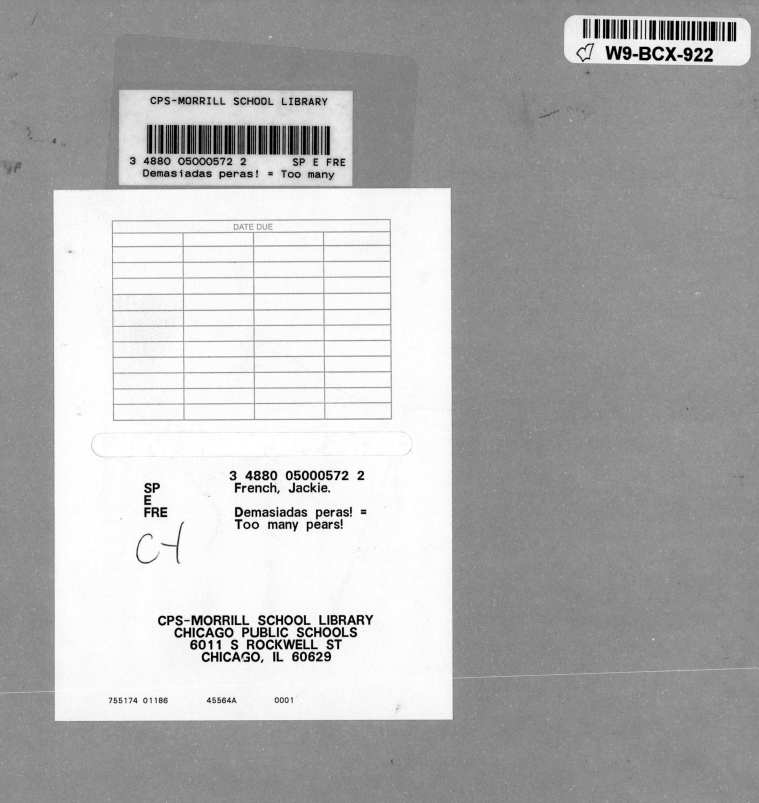

DATE DUE

OP
E
Fre
C-$11.86

¡Demasiadas peras!

Too many pears!

Para Pam Horsey quien ama las peras
casi tanto como Pamela — J.F.

Para Ellyn y Ben — B.W.

To Pam Horsey who loves pears
almost as much as Pamela—J.E.

For Ellyn and Ben—B.W.

Published in the United States of America by Star Bright Books, New York.
Please visit www.starbrightbooks.com.
First published simultaneously in English in the US by
Star Bright Books and in Australia by Koala Books in 2003.

The name Star Bright Books is a registered trademark of Star Bright Books, Inc.
Printed in China 9 8 7 6 5 4 3 2 1

Bilingual edition first published in 2004
Hardback ISBN: 1-59572-012-X   Paperback ISBN: 1-59572-013-8

Translated by Eurotext Translations, Rosetta Stone.

Library of Congress Cataloging-in-Publication Data

Jackie French • Bruce Whatley

¡Demasiadas peras!
Too many pears!

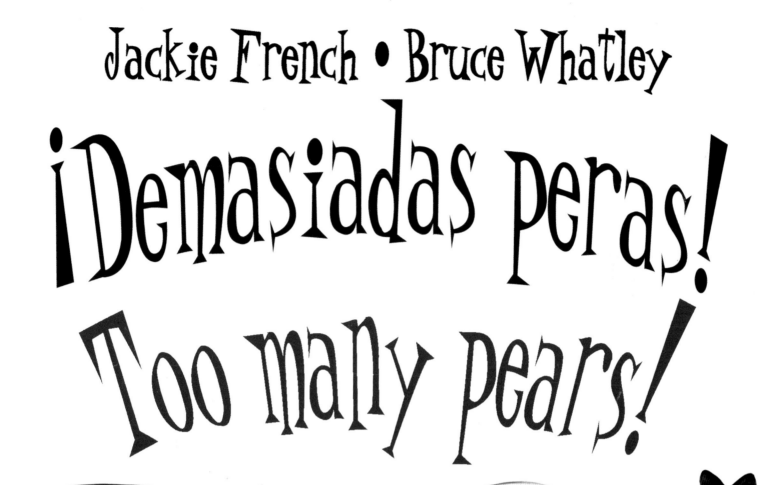

Star Bright Books

New York

A Pamela le gustaban las peras.

Pamela liked pears.

A Pamela le gustaban
las peras frescas.

Pamela liked fresh pears.

¡Le gustaban las peras
más que a Amy!

She liked pears
even more than
Amy did!

A Pamela le gustaba comer peras en el almuerzo.

Pamela liked pears for lunch.

A Pamela le gustaba comer peras
en las meriendas campestres.

Pamela liked pears on picnics.

A Pamela también le gustaba
la compota de peras con helado.

Pamela liked stewed pears
with ice cream too.

A Pamela le gustaba el pastel
de peras con crema batida.

Pamela liked pear pie
and whipped cream.

A Pamela le gustaba recoger peras.

A Amy y a la abuela también.

"¡Tenemos que cuidar nuestras peras!", se
quejaba Amy. "¡Las peras son mis preferidas!"

Amy recogía muchas peras.

¡Pero Pamela recogía aún más!

Pamela liked picking pears.

So did Amy and Grandma.

"We have to save our pears!"
cried Amy. "Pears are my favorite!"

Amy picked lots of pears.

But Pamela picked more!

El abuelo construyó una cerca
alrededor del peral.

Pero Pamela se escurrió debajo de la
cerca por el hoyo de un wombat.

Grandpa built a fence
around the pear tree.

But Pamela crawled through
a wombat hole under the fence.

La abuela tuvo que amarrar a
Pamela a un árbol.

Pero Pamela lo arrancó y se lo llevó
consigo a comer peras.

Grandma tied Pamela up.

But Pamela took the tree
pear-picking too.

"¡Nunca tendremos peras!",
se lamentaban todos.

"Yo sé qué hacer", exclamó Amy.

"We'll never get any pears!"
everyone moaned.

"I know what to do,"
declared Amy.

Amy puso la mesa para Pamela.

Amy set the table for Pamela.

Sirvió peras marrones y peras verdes. Sirvió peras amarillas y peras rojas.

There were brown pears and green pears. There were yellow pears and red pears.

Sirvió peras con jarabe de chocolate. Sirvió peras asadas y pastel de crema con peras y una bandeja con una torre de peras tan alta que llegaba hasta el techo.

There were pears in chocolate sauce. There were baked pears and pear creamcake and a dish of pears a high as the roof!

Pamela sonrió.

Pamela smiled.

Pamela comió una pera.

Pamela ate one pear.

Y luego otra…

Then she ate another pear…

…y otra…

…and another….

...y otra...

...and another...

...y otra...

...and another...

...y otra...

...and another...

...y otra...

...and another...

Pamela devoró 600 peras.
Y luego se detuvo.

Pamela ya no sonreía.

Pamela ate 600 pears.
And then she stopped.

Pamela wasn't smiling any more.

Al día siguiente, el abuelo dejó suelta a Pamela.

"Mira qué hermosas peras,
Pamela", dijo el abuelo.

The next day Grandpa
opened the gate for Pamela.

"Look at all the lovely pears,
Pamela," Grandpa said.

Pero Pamela ya no estaba interesada en las peras.

Pamela wasn't interested.

¡Pamela estaba contemplando
las manzanas!

Pamela was gazing at
the apples!